Sm Little dge

Lionel Le Néouanic

My thanks to Leo Lionni,
Joan Miró, Henri Matisse,
Paul Cox, Annie and Brigitte

First published in France under the title 'Petite Tache'
© Editions du Panama, 2005.

First American edition published in 2006
by Boxer Books Limited.
www.boxerbooks.com

Distributed in the United States and Canada by
Sterling Publishing Co., Inc.
387 Park Avenue South, New York, NY 10016-8810

Text and illustrations copyright © 2005 Lionel Le Néouanic

The rights of Lionel Le Néouanic to be identified as the author and
illustrator of this work have been asserted by him in accordance
with the Copyright, Designs and Patents Act, 1988.

Hardback ISBN 10: 1-905417-22-5
Hardback ISBN 13: 978-1-905417-22-3

Printed in China

Little Smudge is bored, all alone in the corner.

Mommy Smudge says,

"Little Smudge, why are you all alone?
Why don't you go and find some friends?"

So Little Smudge goes to look for some friends.

Little Smudge looks here.

Little Smudge looks there.

Little Smudge looks elsewhere.

Little Smudge looks everywhere and cannot find a single friend.
Suddenly, Little Smudge hears some shouting.

Some little shapes are having an argument about which game to play. There is Little Square, Little Circle, Little Triangle, Little Rectangle and Little Diamond.

Little Smudge gets closer and asks shyly,

"Hello. May I play with you?"

"Have you seen yourself?" asks Little Square.

"You're shapeless!" says Little Triangle.

"You're so ugly!" says Little Circle.

"You're hopeless!" says Little Rectangle.

"Yeah!" says Little Diamond. "You're not like us!"

And they all start shouting,

"Go away, dirty smudge, go away!"

Little Smudge goes home in tears and tells Mommy and Daddy Smudge everything. Still crying, Little Smudge says, "I should have stayed all alone in my corner. I'm so useless and ugly. I'll never have any friends."

Mommy Smudge gives Little Smudge a big, comforting hug, and Daddy Smudge says, **"Don't worry, little one. Of course you'll make friends."**

"You don't know it yet but you have the power to do wonderful things. Listen, and I'll explain it to you..."

Daddy Smudge talks for a long long time. At last he says,
"So Little Smudge, now you know. Go back to those rascals and show them what you can do."

Trembling, Little Smudge goes back to see the little shapes.

"You again!" shouts Little Square
when he sees Little Smudge.
"If you want a fight,
we'll give you a fight!"
threatens Little Triangle.
"Wait," replies Little Smudge,
"I've got something to show you!"

Oh,

Little Smudge has changed into...

"A monster, help!"

cry the other shapes as they flee in all directions.

"Come back

don't be scared!"

incre

Little Smudge can turn into anything.

The little shapes are very impressed.

"May we play with you?" asks a very ashamed Little Square.

"Oh, please, tell us how you do it!" they all cry.

dible!

"Listen,
and I'll
explain it
to you!"

And Little Smudge tells the little shapes
how to transform themselves.

ow! What fun, Little Smudge!

Yippee!

The little friends are having
so much fun that they don't want to leave.

But night is falling. It's time to go home.
Little Smudge hugs his new friends, one by one.

"Goodnight friends!"

says Little Smudge.
"Tomorrow we'll play again.
See you then!"